For Dylan, with all my love x
~T C

For Karyn Anderton
~T M

Copyright © 2011 by Good Books, Intercourse, PA 17534

International Standard Book Number: 978-1-56148-710-3

Library of Congress Catalog Card Number: 2010031243

Text copyright © Tracey Corderoy 2011
Illustrations copyright © Tina Macnaughton 2011
Original edition published in English by Little Tiger Press,
an imprint of Magi Publications, London, England, 2011

LTP/1800/0138/1010 • Printed in China

Library of Congress Cataloging-in-Publication Data

Corderoy, Tracey.
Oh, Dylan! / Tracey Corderoy ; [illustrations] Tina Macnaughton.
p. cm.
Summary: Mommy Duck takes her four ducklings for a spring-time walk,
cautioning them to hold onto the daisy chain they have made, but while
Polly, Molly, and Holly obey, Dylan keeps getting distracted and going astray.
ISBN 978-1-56148-710-3
[1. Ducks--Fiction. 2. Animals--Infancy--Fiction. 3. Obedience--Fiction.]
I. Macnaughton, Tina, ill. II. Title.

PZ7.C815354Oh 2011
[E]--dc22
2010031243

Oh, Dylan!

Tracey Corderoy • Tina Macnaughton

Intercourse, PA 17534, 800/762-7171, www.GoodBooks.com

One breezy day, four little ducklings were making a daisy chain.

"Pick and thread!" chanted Polly, Molly and Holly.

"Look at me!" chuckled Dylan, all tied up in a big flowery knot.

"Now," said Mommy, "we're off to the pond for your very first swim. Hold on to the daisy chain and then you won't get lost."

"It's a choo-choo chain!" cried Dylan. "Choo-choo!"

Polly, Molly, Holly and Dylan skipped along behind
Mommy, singing a springtime song . . .

"Four little ducklings all in a row,
Skipping across the bridge we go!
Wiggle our tails — we're on our way
Down to the pond to splash and play!"

Suddenly, the ducklings spotted a beautiful, blue feather.

"So pretty!" gasped Polly, Molly and Holly.

"Come back!" cried Dylan as the feather blew away.

Then he had a *wonderful* idea . . .

On the other side of the bridge,
some baby lambs were playing
catch-the-petals.

"*We* want to play, too!" said Polly.

"All right," smiled Mommy. She
counted her ducklings as they hopped off
the bridge. "Polly, Molly, Holly and . . .

"OH, MY!" she gasped.
"Where's Dylan?"

All in a fluster
and a flap, everyone
searched for Dylan.

Suddenly, Molly spotted him stuck up a tree!
"Surprise!" cried Dylan. "I got the pretty
feather for you!"

"Oh, *Dylan*," said Mommy. "You *are* a sweetie!
But what did I say about not getting lost?
Now hold on to the choo-choo chain."
"And don't let go!" quacked Polly.

On they went into the woods, singing their song . . .

"*Four little ducklings all in a row,*
Counting the flowers as we go!
Flutter our wings—we're on our way
Down to the pond to dive and play!"

"Mmmm, *lovely!*" cried the sisters, sniffing the flowers.
"A-ccchhhoooo!" sneezed Dylan.
Then he had a *wonderful* idea . . .

At the top of a hill, some baby hedgehogs were playing roly-poly!

"*We* want to roll, too!" said Polly.

"All right," smiled Mommy. She counted her ducklings as they tumbled down the hill. "Polly, Molly, Holly and . . .

"WAIT!" she flapped. "Where's Dylan?"

With wings a-flutter and
feathers flying, everyone
searched for Dylan.
Then suddenly a whirlwind of
fluff came spinning towards them . . .

"Surprise!" cried Dylan. "I picked some pretty flowers for you!"

"Oh, *Dylan*," said Mommy. "You *are* kind! But you forgot what I told you *again* . . ."

"Don't let go of the daisy chain!" yelled his sisters.

On they waddled, under a hedge and *at last* they saw . . .

. . . the pond!

"*Phew!*" gasped Mommy.

"All safely here!"

Polly, Molly and Holly dipped their
toes into the water.

"But it's *c-c-cold*!" they shivered.

"We don't like it!"

Then suddenly,

splash!

Dylan was in . . .

. . . and – *wow* – this was *fun*!

"Look!" cried Dylan. "Look at me!"

He splished and splashed and swam and swam until, all too soon, it was time to go.

On the way home, Dylan felt so very clever. He could *swim*, and Mommy had said he was great! He yawned as a big, silver moon lit the sky. Then he and his sisters sang one final song . . .

"Four sleepy ducklings all in a row,
Waddling back for supper we go.
Tiny stars begin to peep,
Soon we'll all be fast asleep . . . "

When they got home, Mommy baked something warm and tasty. Then she counted her ducklings around the table.

"Polly, Molly, Holly and . . . Oh *dear*," she sighed. "Not again! *Where's Dylan?*"

Polly wriggled, Molly giggled, but Holly
whispered in Mommy's ear. They peeped
around the door . . .

. . . and there, curled up in his
choo-choo chain, was *Dylan*.
   "Nighty-night," giggled Polly,
Molly and Holly as he gave
a tiny snore.
   "Sleep tight," whispered Mommy.
"Sweet dreams!"